César Chávez

Ted O'Hare

Bethany, Missouri

Photo Credits:
All Images © Walter Reutiter Library Wayne State University

Cataloging-in-Publication Data

O'Hare, Ted, 1961-
    Cesar Chavez / Ted O'Hare. — 1st ed.
    p. cm. — (American biographies)

    Includes bibliographical references and index.
    Summary: Introduces the life and accomplishments
of this great Mexican American and labor leader.
    ISBN-13: 978-1-4242-1346-7 (lib. bdg. : alk. paper)
    ISBN-10: 1-4242-1346-0 (lib. bdg. : alk. paper)
    ISBN-13: 978-1-4242-1436-5 (pbk. : alk. paper)
    ISBN-10: 1-4242-1436-X (pbk. : alk. paper)

    1. Chavez, Cesar, 1927-1993—Juvenile literature.
2. Labor leaders—United States—Biography—
uvenile literature. 3. United Farm Workers—History—
Juvenile literature. [1. Chavez, Cesar, 1927-1993.
2. Mexican Americans—Biography. 3. Labor leaders.
 4. Migrant labor. 5. United Farm Workers.
6. Agricultural laborers. 7. Labor unions.]
 I. O'Hare, Ted, 1961- II. Title.
III. Series.
    HD6509.C48O43 2007
    331.88'13'092—dc22

First edition
© 2007 Fitzgerald Books
802 N. 41st Street, P.O. Box 505
Bethany, MO 64424, U.S.A.
Printed in China
Library of Congress Control Number: 2007900245

Table of Contents

An American Leader

César Estrada Chávez was an American farm worker. He was also a labor leader and a civil rights activist.

Chávez was born in 1927 in Arizona and died there in 1993.

Chávez was one of the most admired people of the twentieth century. His efforts on behalf of **migrant** workers made him a hero in the Mexican-American community.

7

Young César

Chávez's mother and grandparents were born in Mexico. They moved to the United States before César was born.

César's father, Librado, worked on a farm, but he also opened a store. The family spoke only Spanish at home.

9

César went to school as a young boy, but he didn't go beyond the eighth grade. The family moved a lot, and César told people he had gone to between 30 and 65 different schools.

Young César found school difficult. He didn't speak English, and that was the only language that was taught in schools.

To California

In the 1930s, the Chávez family lost its farm and moved to California. There they became migrant workers. They helped to harvest crops for many different farms.

During World War II, Chávez joined the Navy.
When the war ended in 1945, he went back to
California and again worked picking crops. In
1948, Chávez married Helen Fabela. They had
eight children.

Making a Better Life

During the 1950s and 1960s, Chávez worked to make life better for field workers. He got the workers together and formed a **union**.

He got grape pickers to **strike** in 1965, because he felt they were not being paid a fair wage. For this reason, Chávez asked Americans to **boycott** grapes.

Chávez became a **spokesman** and founder of the United Farm Workers. He also led **protests** to support his beliefs. Several times he organized **hunger strikes**.

Like the statesman of India, Mahatma Gandhi, Chávez believed in **nonviolence** to get his message across.

A Hero to Mexican Americans

Most farm workers today benefit from Chávez's actions. They are paid and treated better than they were in the past.

For these reasons, Chávez is a hero to many Mexican Americans.

Chávez died in 1993. In 1994, President Bill Clinton gave him the Presidential Medal of Freedom. The United States honored Chávez by putting his image on a postage stamp in 2003.

Many schools, parks, and streets have been named after him. Several states celebrate Chávez's birthday as a state holiday.

Dates to Remember

1927   César Chávez born near Yuma, Arizona,
        on March 31
1946   César Chávez returns from World War II
1948   César marries Helen Fabela
1965   Chávez asks grape pickers to strike for
        better working conditions
1993   César Chávez dies, April 23
1994   Chávez is awarded the Presidential
        Medal of Freedom

Glossary

boycott (BOY kot) — to refuse to buy or use something

hunger strikes (HUNG ur STRYKZ) — refusing to eat as a protest

migrant (MY grunt) — someone who moves from place to place

nonviolence (non VY uh luntz) — protesting without violence

protests (PRO tests) — demonstrations against something

spokesman (SPOKES mun) — a leader of a group

strike (STRYK) — a refusal to work until certain demands are met

union (YOON yun) — workers who join together to get better conditions

Index

FURTHER READING

Del Castillo, Richard Griswold. *César Chávez: The Struggle for Justice/César Chávez: La lucha por la justicia (Bilingual edition).* Piñata Books, 2002.

Krull, Kathleen. *Harvesting Hope: The Story of Cesar Chavez.* Harcourt Brace Children's Books, 2003.

Perez, L. King. *First Day in Grapes.* Aladdin Books, 2003.

Wadsworth, Ginger. *Cesar Chavez.* Carolrhoda Books, 2005.

WEBSITES TO VISIT

Because Internet links change so often, Fitzgerald Books has developed an online list of websites related to the subject of this book. This site is updated regularly. Please use this link to access the list: www.fitzgeraldbookslinks.com/ab/cc

ABOUT THE AUTHOR

Ted O'Hare is an author and editor of children's nonfiction books. Ted has written over fifty children's books over the past decade. Ted has worked for many publishing houses including the Macmillan Children's Book Group.